THE ADVENTURES OF
MAVERICK
THE HOCKEY PLAYER
ALEX THE GOALIE

BY **GINA USUFZY** &
ABDUL USUFZY

ILLUSTRATED BY JASON VELAZQUEZ

Alex the Goalie
By Gina and Abdul Usufzy
Illustrated by Jason Velazquez

Printed in the United States of America.
ISBN-13: 979-8-9884137-2-1

CSIT Publishing
Las Vegas, Nevada

In Loving Memory of Alex Bush #29.

Image on the left

Alex trying on Jakes gear for a try goalie event.

"That was a great practice." Maverick told his friend Alex.

"Yeah, I guess." Alex sighed.

Maverick saw Alex's frown.

"Is something wrong, Alex?"

"No." Alex replied but Maverick did not believe him.

"Are you sure?" Maverick asked.

"Well, there's a big goalie event coming up and I really want to try it out." Alex replied. "A goalie?" Maverick asked. He shook his head. "I don't think I would want to have pucks shot at me for the whole game." Alex laughed. "I think it would be awesome to stop the other team from scoring." Maverick shrugged. "Then you should go." "I can't." Alex replied. He stared at the ground. "My parents can't afford goalie gear."

Maverick thought for a moment then had an idea. "Maybe my brother's goalie gear will fit you."

"Do you think Jake would let me use it?" Alex asked with excitement.

Maverick shrugged. "It doesn't fit him so I don't see why you couldn't use it. Come on." Maverick tightened his grip on his bag and ran up to his mom. "Mom, can Alex try on Jake's goalie gear?"

Before his mom could reply, he added, "He really wants to try the goalie event coming up but his parents can't buy him the gear and Jake doesn't use it anymore."

"Well, Jake's gear may be a little big but he can try it on." His mom replied.

The next day, Alex's dad brought him to Maverick's house so he could try on the goalie gear. "Perfect fit!" Maverick exclaimed.

"Not quite." Alex's dad replied. He shook the gear a little to show how loose it was on Alex.

"Will it work for the goalie event?" Maverick's mom asked.

Alex's dad set his chin on his hand and let out a deep breath. He smiled and nodded. "I think so." He replied.

Maverick and Alex high-fived each other.

At the goalie event, Maverick, his mom, and Alex's dad were sitting in the stands. Every time Alex stopped the puck they jumped up and cheered for him.

"Great job!" Maverick cheered.

"Way to go, Alex!" Alex's dad yelled and clapped his hands.

Alex was having a really great time being a goalie.

A few days later, Maverick and Alex were in the locker room after practice. "I have to figure out how to get some goalie gear." Alex told Maverick.

"What for?" Maverick asked, "The goalie event won't happen again for another year."

"I know but I want to be a goalie." Alex replied.

"I'm sure my mom will let you use Jake's gear again."

Alex shook his head. "It's a little loose and my dad said that won't be good for regular games. I could get hurt."

"Maybe we can raise some money and buy you the gear." Maverick replied.

"How would we do that?" Alex asked.

"My cousin sold some baseball cards and got some money." Maverick said. "Do you have any baseball cards?"

"No." Alex replied.

"I saw this kid on TV who had a lemonade stand and raised a bunch of money. We could sell lemonade."

"I don't know how to make lemonade." Alex replied.

"Neither do I." Maverick added.

"Does he need to borrow Jake's old gear again?" Mom asked.

"No, he needs to buy his own gear because he wants to be a goalie." Maverick replied.

"Oh." Mom nodded. "Yes, he will need his own gear then."

"But his parents still can't afford gear so we are trying to think of a way for him to make money." Maverick replied. "Do you think you could go on the computer and ask your people to help?"

"Ask my people?" Mom asked.

"You know, the people that help kids with their hockey gear."

Maverick stood next to mom as she sat down at the computer.

"I can make a post that there is a player in need of goalie gear and see if anyone can help Alex out." Mom said.

"Yes, let's do that!" Maverick jumped up and fisted bumped the air. "Alex is going to be so excited."

"Well, nobody has given anything yet so let's not get too excited." Mom replied.

Day after day, Maverick asked his mom if anyone had replied to her post.

"No, I haven't had anyone reply to the post yet." Mom replied.

"Ok." Maverick would reply and try to come up with other ways they might be able to raise the money.

Then one day after school, Mom greeted him at the door. "Maverick, guess what?"
"What?" Maverick asked.
"I got a phone call today while you were in school from a family who donated a whole set of goalie gear to the foundation for Alex!"
"No way!" Maverick shouted in excitement!
"I picked up the gear today and called Alex's dad. They are going to meet us this evening so he can try it on."
"Oh, mom, I hope it fits him." Maverick said.
"I hope so to, Maverick." Mom replied.

Later that evening, Maverick and his mom met Alex and his dad at the rink. Alex tried on all the goalie gear and to everyone's surprise it fit him perfectly.

"Can we try it out on the ice?" Maverick asked.

"Maverick, you're going to shoot pucks at your friend?" Mom asked with concern.

"Don't worry, he won't get them past me." Alex said. He patted his new gear and laughed.

"Challenge accepted!" Maverick said. He smiled and skated out onto the ice with Alex.

Meet the Authors

Gina and Abdul Usufzy are happily married and live in North Las Vegas, Nevada with their three children. Aside from running a local hockey league, the Usufzys run Jake Kielb's Hockey Foundation, a non-profit in Las Vegas dedicated to supporting and growing youth hockey in their local community.

Up Next in the Adventures with Maverick the Hockey Player series.

Made in the USA
Las Vegas, NV
04 February 2024